It's Payback Time

JAN WEEKS

Illustrated by Steven Bray

sundance
A Haights Cross Communications Company

The Story Characters

Daniel
That's me.

Luke and Chris
The terrible
Perkins twins.

Nancy
The sister of the
Perkins twins.

The Story Setting

Twins' House

Daniel's House

Genie's Bottle

Store

3

TABLE OF CONTENTS

CHAPTER 1

Two Against One

I used to like going to our beach house. Then the Perkins twins moved in next door.

Mr. and Mrs. Perkins are OK. Mr. Perkins rides a motorcycle. Sometimes he gives me a ride.

It's their terrible twins, Luke and Chris, that I can't stand.

"Give me your boogie board, Daniel," Luke says, when he sees me on the beach. "If you don't, I'll flatten your nose and punch your lights out."

Chris doesn't even bother to say anything to me. He just grabs my board and runs into the water, laughing. If I try to get it back, he pushes me under the waves. Then he sits on me.

Their boogie boards look like they came from the dump. By the time they get through with mine, it will look the same. There are already scratches on it and big pieces missing from the sides.

Nancy is the twins' little sister. She would like to hang around me all of the time. "Can I play with Daniel?" she asks my mom at least a million times a day.

Good old Mom. She tries to help.
"I think Daniel is busy right now," she
always answers.

Then Nancy says, "Can I come in and
wait?"

Being loved by Nancy is almost as bad as being bullied by her brothers.

CHAPTER 2

Ruckus Is Missing!

The Perkins have a dog called Ruckus. Yesterday someone let Ruckus off his leash. Nobody knew where he'd gone.

Mr. Perkins needs Ruckus to guard his motorcycle. He said the twins should have tied him up properly. So they had to go look for him.

The twins spent hours climbing the hills and calling the dog's name. But they didn't find him.

When they came back, the twins
blamed me. They thought I let Ruckus
off his leash. That's because I told
Nancy I don't like their dog. He's
always barking at me.

"I didn't touch your silly dog," I said
to them. "He must have chewed
through the rope."

"Your sneaker was near his doghouse. That means it had to be you," Chris answered.

As if that were proof! Ruckus was always taking things.

Later, Dad asked me to go to the store to get some bread. Chris and Luke were coming back from the beach. They had found Ruckus. The three of them chased me all the way home.

"You come back here!" they shouted.

I had to think of a way to pay them back.

CHAPTER 3

Beachcombing

Today the sun was shining, so I headed down to the beach. There was a lot of seaweed and junk washed up on the sand.

I was dragging a stick behind me when it hit something hard. I looked down and saw a shiny object in the sand.

It was a green, metal bottle. It was round at the bottom and had a long, skinny neck. I unscrewed the lid.

moke floated out and formed a shape
next to me. The shape turned into a
little man.

My mouth fell open. I couldn't believe
my eyes. I'd found a bottle with a
genie in it!

CHAPTER 4

Are You Really a Genie?

The little man didn't look like a genie.
"What are you staring at?" he asked,
folding his arms and glaring at me.

"Are you really a genie?" I asked.

"You saw me come out of the bottle, didn't you?" he replied. "Why are you bothering me? I've been in that bottle for a thousand years, and I have things to do."

I had set the genie free. Wasn't he supposed to grant me three wishes? "I am your master now," I said. "You must do what I tell you."

'Who told you that?" he said, as he laughed at me.

"Everyone knows that a genie must obey his master," I said.

"Nobody told me that," answered the
genie, "so, good-bye!" And with that,
he floated back into the bottle.

I turned the bottle upside down and shook it.

"Go away!" he shouted. "You're making me dizzy."

"You'd better come out," I told him. "If you don't, I'll fill your bottle with water."

"Put me down," he answered. "Or I'll turn you into a three-headed toad and feed you to the sharks."

"You can't do that to me," I said. "I am your master!"

"Oh, very well," he sighed. "You can have one wish."

CHAPTER 5

The Wish

"Come on! Make it snappy," grumbled the genie. "I don't have all day."

I made up my mind. I wanted him to make me invisible.

Shazam!

looked down. Where my body used to be, there was nothing! No legs, no body, no arms. Was this how a ghost felt?

I raced home singing, "Hi ho! Hi ho! No one can see where I go. And when you can't be seen, no one can see where you've been."

Dad was in the backyard hanging out
the towels. I decided to have some
fun. When Dad turned to grab
clothespins, I threw the towels back
into the basket.

When he went to tell Mom what had happened, I hung up all of the towels.

"Maybe you should stay out of the sun," Mom said to Dad. "I think you are seeing things."

When she went back inside, I sprayed Dad with the hose. He went inside mumbling to himself.

I could hear Ruckus barking. He was tied up under a tree. I gently pulled his tail. He ran around in circles.

I bounced his ball in front of him.
I crawled inside his doghouse and
banged on it from the inside.

Ruckus lay down and put his paws
over his eyes.

Inside their house, the Perkins kids were having lunch. They all had glasses of juice. Luke drank his in one gulp.

I poured Chris's juice into Luke's glass.
When Chris saw that his glass was
empty, he grabbed Luke's full one. It
slipped and juice went all over Nancy's
spaghetti.

Nancy screamed, "Mom, look what Chris did!"

Mrs. Perkins went to get Nancy another lunch.

I then tipped Luke's spaghetti over his head. It looked like red worms.

Luke thought that Chris had done it. He got up and started to fight with Chris. Luke shoved Chris. Chris shoved him back. They were both yelling.

"Go to your bedroom," Mr. Perkins roared. "And stay there until I tell you to come out."

It was the most fun I'd had in ages!

CHAPTER 6

Time to Go Home

At my house, we were having pizza. It smelled good! Mom had cut a slice for me, but I couldn't eat it . . . not while Mom and Dad were sitting there.

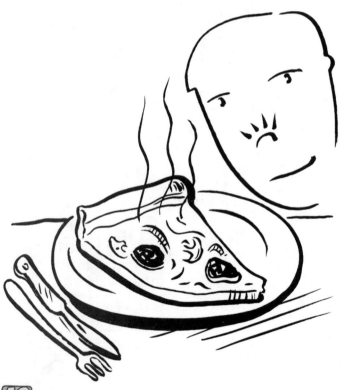

I was really hungry! I waited until they weren't looking and took a big bite. It tasted so good that I took another bite.

"Why are you eating Daniel's pizza?" Mom asked Dad.

"I'm not," Dad answered, shaking his head. "I don't believe the things that are happening today."

"I wonder where Daniel can be," Mom said. "It's not like him to miss pizza. I hope nothing has happened to him."

Later that day, they really began to
worry about me. They went next door.
The Perkins twins didn't want to help
search for me.

"Who cares if he's lost?" they
grumbled.

I followed Mom and Dad to the beach. They were sad and upset. I was sorry for the tricks that I'd played on them while I was invisible. I was even sorry for what I'd done to the Perkins kids.

They hadn't gone far when Chris
found the genie's bottle. "Catch, Luke,"
he said, throwing it to his brother.

"I bet I can throw it higher than you can," Luke said, tossing up the bottle.

"Bet you can't!"

I had to do something. I had to get
that bottle back before they opened it.
I was afraid that I might never become
visible again. Quickly snatching it
from Chris, I raced along the beach.
I unscrewed the lid.

I don't want to be invisible anymore," shouted down the neck of the bottle.

"Too bad," the genie answered. "That was your wish. Go away."

"You have to help me," I sobbed. "Please, Genie."

The genie poked his head out of the bottle. "Very well," he said. "You can have a second wish. But only if you promise to throw my bottle back into the ocean."

I promised.

He did his trick, and I was visible
again. I could see me again . . . my
legs, my arms, everything!

The little man went back into his
bottle. I put the lid on and climbed up
onto some rocks. Then I threw the
bottle far out to sea.

'om and Dad came running over to ne. After they hugged and kissed me, got into big trouble for making them worry. I didn't care. I was just happy to be back.

GLOSSARY

beachcombing
hunting for good things (treasure) on a beach

boogie board
a small, foam surf board

genie
a magic person who lives in a bottle

grumbled
complained in a low, cranky voice

guard
to look after

invisible
something that is there
but cannot be seen

obey
to do what you
are told

visible
something that
can be seen

Talking with the Author and the Illustrator

Jan Weeks (author)

Who is your favorite cartoon character?
   The Road Runner.

If you could go anywhere, where would it be?
   Scotland, in the summer.

What are three things that you can't live without?
   A kind word, a friendly smile, and an
   unlimited supply of fattening food.

Steven Bray (illustrator)

Who is your favorite cartoon character?
   Homer Simpson.

Why is the sky blue?
   Because white clouds look best against blue.

What are three things that you can't live without?
   Clean socks, daydreaming, and coffee.

Copyright © 2002 Sundance Publishing

All rights reserved. No part of this publication may be
reproduced, stored in a retrieval system or transmitted
in any form or by any means, electronic, mechanical,
photocopying, recording, or otherwise, without the prior
written permission of the publisher.

Published by Sundance Publishing
P.O. Box 1326, 234 Taylor Street, Littleton, MA 01460
800-343-8204

Copyright © text Jan Weeks
Copyright © illustrations Steven Bray

First published 1999 as Sparklers by
Blake Education, Locked Bag 2022, Glebe 2037, Australia
Exclusive United States Distribution: Sundance Publishing

ISBN 0-7608-8140-9

Printed in Canada